A Tiny Miracle

Richard M. Wainwright
Illustrated by Jack Crompton

FAMILY
LIFE
PUBLISHING

Dedicated to our Parents

R.W   J.C

Published by Family Life Publishing
Dennis, MA 02638

Printed in Singapore by Tien Wah Press
Published in the United States of America 1986

A Tiny Miracle

Richard M. Wainwright
Illustrated by Jack Crompton

FAMILY
LIFE
PUBLISHING

Best wishes,

Richard M. Wainwright

Happy Birthday

April 10, 1990

WAY UP NORTH, the tallest, oldest and wisest oak tree was the first to hear the unfamiliar sounds. All the trees and creatures of the valley looked and waited to see who and what was coming into their valley.

Soon two strong horses pulling a wagon came into view. An old man held the reins and a small young boy sat closely beside him. The back of the wagon was filled with seedlings. They had come to the valley to plant baby Christmas trees.

"Whoa," called the old man, and the horses willingly came to a stop beside the oldest and wisest oak. Climbing down from the wagon, the old man took the little boy in his arms. Reaching into the wagon, he picked up his long-handled shovel and one by one began planting the little Christmas trees.

By the time the sun was ready to leave the valley the old man had finished. "Wait, grampa," shouted the little boy, "here is a small seedling that fell out of the wagon and hasn't been planted."

"I'm afraid that tiny seedling will never grow big and beautiful," replied his grandfather, "but if you want to you can plant it, and it will be your tree. If the tree lives, I will sell it for you." The little boy eagerly took the big shovel from his grandfather. It wasn't easy for him to use, but after several tries he had dug a little hole under the branches of the oldest and wisest oak. Carefully, his small hands placed the tiny seedling in the hole and covered its roots with dirt. The old man smiled and gently lifted his grandson onto the wagon seat. Then he climbed up beside the boy, took the reins and headed the horses out of the valley.

"Hello there, little one," boomed the wise old oak.

The tiny Christmas tree bent way back looking up toward the deep voice and replied, "Gosh, you're awfully tall. I'm glad to be here near you. I was lucky the little boy saw me, or I never would have had the chance to grow into a big, beautiful Christmas tree." Darkness came quickly to the valley, the tiny Christmas tree wished everyone good night and he drifted off to sleep.

Each day the tiny Christmas tree eagerly awaited the warmth of the sun's rays, yet because the little boy had planted him on the west side of the old oak a giant shadow covered him most of the day. The wise old oak sadly watched his little friend anxiously wait for the morning sun. The tiny Christmas tree could easily see that the sun shone on his brothers and sisters all day long, but it was only at sunset, the very last moments of the day, that the rays of the sun reached him. He was happy and thankful for these minutes in the sun. Even on days when the sun didn't shine the tiny Christmas tree was the merriest and happiest of all the Christmas trees in the valley.

When clouds approached he sang about how everyone was growing and how wonderful it was to feel the fresh raindrops. The tiny Christmas tree heard more raindrops fall on the leaves and branches of the mighty oak than fell on his tiny needles. He could

see the rain falling all over the valley, while only a few drops trickled onto his tiny branches. Yet, these few droplets made him very happy, and he sang, "I'm growing, I'm growing."

Cool Spring breezes were followed by hot summer days and in turn gave way to chilly nights signaling the beginning of autumn. "Look at me—look at me," shouted the Christmas trees to each other. Since being planted in the valley, all the other Christmas trees

had received lots of sun and water during their first spring and summer, and now after several months each tree could see how much it had grown. "I'm six inches taller and five inches fuller." "Me too—me too," they chorused.

All the trees had grown a great deal—all except the tiny Christmas tree. He was healthy from his several minutes of sunshine each day and the few drops of water that found their way to his tiny roots when it rained, but he hadn't received enough sun and water to grow much bigger. He didn't realize this was the reason he hadn't grown much—only the wise old oak understood.

"I'm sure next year I'll grow faster," the tiny Christmas tree thought.

Many quiet snowy days passed before spring and summer came again. As always the tiny Christmas tree was merry and friendly from sunrise to sunset, greeting all creatures who came nearby. He loved all the animals in the valley—especially their babies, who snuggled under his small branches or hid behind him when they were playing games. He was always cheerful and happy, always—until fall came and the other Christmas trees once again told each other how much they had grown during the summer and the tiny Christmas tree could see how little he had grown. Each year he told himself that he would grow faster the following summer. His little animal friends assured him that he would grow more next year. They knew he worried about his small size and they all loved him.

During the seventh summer there was great excitement amongst the Christmas trees as they knew the Christmas tree grower would return in the fall. The mighty oak's leaves began to turn orange and then fall to the ground. The tiny Christmas tree wondered if he too would somehow be chosen. No one could say he wasn't perfectly shaped, but he was so, so small. His larger brothers and sisters had hardly noticed their relative who had lived under the branches of the wise old oak. For them, their own growth and appearance was all they had thought about.

6

As the wise old oak's last few leaves drifted to the ground, winter's chill was in the air, and soon snow covered the ground. The chirping of a few winter birds and the whispering of the anxiously waiting Christmas trees were the only sounds to be heard. The old oak sadly looked down at his little friend, knowing it wouldn't be long before the tiny Christmas tree would be heart-broken.

Two days later the sounds of horses' hoofs padding quietly in the snow floated into the valley. The time had come to cut the Christmas trees. The old man looked the same, but his grandson seated next to him had grown taller. The boy held the reins and confidently guided the horses towards the Christmas trees. Each Christmas tree had shaken its branches and was standing as tall and straight as it could. This was the day they had been growing for. The old man took an axe and the boy a hatchet from the sleigh, and they began cutting the Christmas trees. They were happy and cheerful as they worked, for they found that all of the seedlings had grown into tall, well-shaped trees.

Up on the slope, covered by a pile of snow because he wasn't strong enough to shake it off, the tiny Christmas tree peeked out and watched the old man and the boy fill the wagon with Christmas trees. He was happy for his bigger brothers and sisters, but he was worried that he might be forgotten. By late in the afternoon, all the Christmas trees had been cut, and the old man and the boy climbed back onto the wagon and prepared to leave the valley.

"I'm here, I'm here," cried the tiny Christmas tree. The old oak above him sadly shook his branches.

Yet, just before the old man had taken the reins, the boy had pointed toward the mighty oak. The old man nodded and headed the team of horses toward the old oak tree. As they came under its branches they stopped and climbed down. "I'm sorry, son, your tree must have died. I don't see it, unless it's bent over under that little pile of snow." The boy rushed over to the snow pile and began brushing the snow off the tiny Christmas tree. "It's not bent over, Grampa, it is just very, very small. I guess you wouldn't be able to sell this tree for me."

"Now wait a minute. Let me take a closer look at your tree. It certainly is the tiniest Christmas tree I have ever seen. However, it is perfectly shaped. Maybe the man from the city will be willing to buy it. Go ahead and cut it." A few minutes later the horses began their journey home with the tiny Christmas tree joyfully nestled between the old man and the boy.

"Good-by, good-by." cried the tiny Christmas tree, and all the animals of the forest appeared to wave. "Good-by, my little friend," boomed the great oak. "We will all miss you, but we know you will make someone's Christmas especially wonderful."

Evening shadows were long when the wagon loaded
with Christmas trees emerged from the forest. The
tired horses were hungry, and they hurried along
looking forward to their supper of hay and oats. At
the top of the hill the old man stopped the horses and
waited while his grandson got down from the wagon
to open a gate. It had been a long exciting day for the
young boy. As he and his grandfather walked past
the wagon full of trees toward the house, he wondered if the man from the city would buy his tiny
Christmas tree.

Looking around from his perch on the driver's seat,
the tiny Christmas tree could see a long, long way.
Nearby, bright lights from other farms twinkled along
the road. Beyond them a cluster of soft lights below

the hills indicated several small villages, and way in the distance a faint glow came from thousands of lights in the city. Of course the tiny Christmas tree didn't know all this. At this moment he simply was the happiest Christmas tree in the wagon. Soon, he thought, he would be part of someone's Christmas.

His bigger brothers and sisters were gaily chatting about how beautiful they would look with brightly-wrapped presents nestled under their needles and sparkling decorations hanging gracefully from their branches. The tiny Christmas tree was content to simply listen to the hopes of the other Christmas trees and watch the lights of villages and the city disappear one by one. Friendly stars appeared, telling him it was time to sleep and dream.

11

The next morning, a large truck drove into the farm. "Good morning, my friends," the truck driver shouted, "I see you have your Christmas trees ready for sale." After he shook hands with the old man and the boy, they all walked over to the wagon to transfer the trees to the truck. Before placing the trees in the truck the driver held each tree up for inspection. "They're fine trees, all right," he commented. After taking the last tree from the sleigh, the truck driver took out his wallet. The old man smiled, took the money and thanked the truck driver. "Before you go," the old man began, "we have one more tree to sell," and he reached up on the wagon seat for the tiny Christmas tree. "This is the boy's tree. He hopes you will buy it from him." For a brief moment the rugged face of the truck driver looked questioningly at the old man; then with a wink and a smile, it changed. "Yes, I certainly would like to buy this little tree. It is very, very small, but it is beautiful." He took some coins from his pocket and handed them to the smiling young boy. "Thank you, sir," the boy replied. "I know someone will want my little Christmas tree."

"People are waiting for me in the city. I had better get going," the truck driver said, as he placed the tiny Christmas tree in the back of the truck with all the other trees. "See you next year," he called, as the old man and the boy waved good-by. The long trip to the city had begun.

At first the dirt road was very bumpy, and the Christmas trees grumbled and complained that if the road was going to be like this all the way to the city their branches would surely break. The tiny Christmas tree was his cheerful self, and he sang as they bumped along the road.

"I don't know why you're happy," said the always grumpy Christmas tree. "You're not big enough to have toys and presents under your branches, and you're not strong enough to hold up lots of decorations—nobody will want you." "Shhhhh! don't be so mean," several of the other trees whispered before the tiny Christmas tree could squeak a reply.

The grumpy Christmas tree said no more. The tiny Christmas tree fell silent. Maybe the grumpy Christmas tree is right, he thought. "No one will want me," and he began to worry.

With a final bump, the truck turned onto a wide paved highway and began to pick up speed. Soon, new sounds captured the attention of the trees. Engines roared, horns honked, and by listening carefully they could hear the tinkling of Christmas bells. Excitement returned and the aches and pains from the rough ride were quickly forgotten. The truck paused, and a policeman waved the driver forward. "Bringing Christmas to the city, I see," he called. "We've been waiting for you."

Tall buildings rose on both sides of the street. A turn here and a turn there, and finally the truck rolled to a stop. Strings of Christmas lights brightly lit a corner lot. In the back of the lot a small house was decorated with holly and Christmas wreaths.

"You're just in time," the jolly owner shouted. "People have been asking me all day when the Christmas trees were coming." Looking into the truck, he first saw the tiny Christmas tree. "Say, I can't buy this tree. It's much too small. No one will buy it." he said.

"Don't worry," the truck driver replied, "I bought it to please a little boy and I won't charge you anything for it." The round little man nodded and took the tiny Christmas tree toward the back of the lot. He disappeared into the little house, and then came out with a hammer and some boards.

Climbing up a short ladder, the stand owner quickly built a shelf and placed the tiny Christmas tree on it. "How does it look?", he called to the truck driver.

"It looks just fine—I'm glad you could find a use for the little tree," he replied.

From his viewpoint the tiny Christmas tree could see the stand owner carefully arranging his bigger brothers and sisters around the lot and hanging price tags from their branches.

Ten days remained before Christmas. Soon people began looking at the Christmas trees. Slowly they wandered from tree to tree—each tree waiting anxiously, hoping to be chosen. "We'll take that one," a tall man called pointing to one of the trees. The happy stand owner quickly removed the price tag from the

tree, accepted some money from his customer, and wished him a Merry Christmas.

"Good-by, good-by," shouted the selected Christmas tree. He waved to his brothers and sisters as the tall man carried him toward the street. "Good-by—have a wonderful Christmas!", all the remaining trees chorused. All, that is, except the grumpy Christmas tree. The grumpy Christmas tree had been placed way back in the lot by the side of the little house, and he only grunted and looked disagreeable when other Christmas trees were sold.

The tiny Christmas tree was once more his happy, cheerful self. He believed that there was still a chance that someone would want him for Christmas. From his perch the tiny Christmas tree could see everything that was going on. He was bursting with the excitement of the season—the sounds and sights of Christmas were all around—and he loved it.

People with musical instruments came to play and sing on the corner. The tiny Christmas tree listened carefully so he could learn the words and tunes. Soon he came to understand the story and the meaning of the word Christmas, and the hope and joy a very special baby had brought the people of the world. It wasn't long before he too was singing, and long after the musicians had left the tiny Christmas tree continued to sing Christmas Carols. He cheered when each Christmas tree was sold, and joined the remaining Christmas trees in wishing the departing tree a "Merry Christmas, and good-by."

On the day before Christmas only two gentle trees remained, along with the grumpy tree. "I hope we will be bought today," one of the gentle trees murmured.

"Maybe you will and maybe you won't," the grumpy tree grumbled. "But I know I will be picked today—just you wait and see."

In the middle of the morning an old man and old woman stopped and picked one of the gentle trees, and later a young man selected the other gentle tree. As the last gentle tree was carried from the lot it was late in the day. The sun had been replaced by a gray sky and fluffy white snow flakes had begun to fall. "Har-ump," said grumpy tree to the tiny Christmas tree, "I'll be leaving you soon, and you will be spending your Christmas all by yourself."

The stand owner turned on the Christmas lights. He hoped to sell the several wreaths and pieces of holly that remained, and the one remaining Christmas tree. A few minutes later a poorly dressed man shuffled toward him. Pausing before the one remaining tree, he hesitatingly asked if the stand owner would sell the last tree for only one dollar. He said that was all the money he had, and his family was hoping he would be able to buy a tree. The stand owner looked into the man's eyes, smiled and sadly nodded his head.

"Take a wreath and some holly, and don't forget the mistletoe," the stand owner replied before reaching into his pocket and taking out several dollars. "And add this money to your dollar and buy another present or two."

The man's eyes brightened and he stood a little straighter as he hoisted the Christmas tree on his shoulder and picked up a wreath, holly and some mistletoe with his other hand. "Thank you very much and a Merry Christmas to you and your family," he called as he disappeared into the night.

It was time for the Christmas tree stand owner to leave and spend the few remaining hours of Christmas Eve with his family. Turning off the lights, he locked the door of his little house. Above him, a tear began to slowly trickle down the branches of the tiny Christmas tree. The grumpy Christmas tree was right. He wasn't going to be part of anyone's Christmas. For the first time in his life, he began to cry. He would not contribute to the joy and happiness of the season. He wasn't wanted. His struggle to live and grow had been for nothing, and he sobbed uncontrollably.

As the stand owner began to walk away, a young man dashed around the corner, knocking them both to the ground. "I'm terribly sorry," the young man said as he helped the stand owner to his feet. "I must find the Christmas tree man — I've got to buy a Christmas tree for my wife."

"Well, my young friend," the stand owner replied, you have found the Christmas tree man, but I am afraid that I sold my last Christmas tree ten minutes ago, and as you can see they are all gone. I am sorry, but I must be going.

"Wait, please wait—isn't that a tree on the roof of your little house? Would you sell that one to me?" the young man asked.

The Christmas tree man man looked up, and said, "I forgot about that little tree. If you climb up there and take it down, it's yours. There is a step ladder beside my little house. Now, I must hurry along. Merry Christmas."

The young man quickly climbed on the roof and carefully detached the tiny Christmas tree. He held it up, smiled, and after jumping to the ground tucked it under his arm and began to run down the street. It had all happened so fast the tiny Christmas tree hardly had time to shake the tears off his branches. A few minutes ago he was alone and unwanted, and now he was flying down the street with someone who was happy to have him. At the corner the young man waved a taxi to the curb. "To the hospital, driver, and as fast as possible," he said. The taxi sped away into the night, coming to a stop ten minutes later in front of a big brick building. The young man paid the taxi driver and wished him a Merry Christmas before dashing up the steps through the front door. Inside all was quiet as he hurried down a long corridor toward a lady dressed in white. "How is my wife?" he asked the nurse.

"A little uncomfortable I am afraid, Mr. Johnson, but that is to be expected," she replied. "You may go in." Mr. Johnson tiptoed into the room. His wife was sleeping, and he quietly placed the tiny Christmas tree on a table near her bed.

A few minutes later Mrs. Johnson opened her eyes and saw the tiny Christmas tree. "It's beautiful, " she cried, "it's just perfect." But after she smiled pain came to her eyes—"I believe it's almost time," she whispered, closing her eyes. A few moments later the nurse entered the room, followed by a man also dressed in white and carrying a small black bag. The doctor asked Mrs. Johnson several questions before saying it was time for her to come with him. Mr. Johnson held his wife's hand as she was wheeled out of the room.

Once again the tiny Christmas tree was alone. Not only was he alone, but he was sad. He had quickly grown to like Mr. and Mrs. Johnson. Mrs. Johnson seemed to be sick, and Mr. Johnson appeared worried, yet at the same time, excited. Although he didn't understand, he hoped with all his might that Mrs. Johnson would get better. He wished he could have been with Mrs. Johnson longer as he seemed to make her happy. All was quiet; then a nearby church's Christmas bells chimed the hour. It would not be long before midnight, which would herald Christmas Day. The tiny Christmas tree wondered what Christmas would be like for him. He wanted so much to make people happy.

Looking toward the hall, the tiny Christmas tree could see Mr. Johnson pacing back and forth. Suddenly he stuck his head into the room and looked at the tiny Christmas tree. Mr. Johnson seemed to get an idea. He put on his coat and hurried away. Soon, he reappeared carrying a large box, which he put on a nearby table. Carefully he began taking miniature Christmas ornaments from the box and gently hanging them on the branches of the tiny Christmas tree. Shining blue, red, and gold balls and silver tinsel soon covered the tiny Christmas tree. Tiny lights were added and began twinkling as Mr. Johnson placed a small gold star at the top of the tiny Christmas tree. Under his branches Mr. Johnson arranged a group of tiny

figures. The tiny Christmas tree looked at the scene below his branches. He saw a cow, a donkey, some sheep and three larger animals with long-robed men sitting on them, and people in a half-circle looking at a little baby, which was lying on some straw.

"What could be happening?", the tiny Christmas tree wondered. "What was the matter with Mrs. Johnson?" Just at that moment the church bells across the street began ringing, announcing to everyone that the most joyous day of the year had arrived. Christ's birthday had begun.

As the sound of the twelfth ring faded into silence, another sound was heard. It was a weak, high-pitched cry, which grew louder and stronger and came closer and closer. The nurse marched into the room, followed closely by a beaming Mr. Johnson. Dr. Jones pushed a rolling bed that contained a tired but happy Mrs. Johnson. Beside her, bundled in a small blue blanket, was a tiny baby. The tiny Christmas tree now understood. "What a wonderful Christmas present for the Johnsons," he thought. Dr. Jones told everyone that Mrs. Johnson needed rest and sleep. The nurse gently took the baby and left with Dr. Jones. Mr. Johnson, still smiling, leaned over the bed and kissed Mrs. Johnson. There was no sign of pain on Mrs. Johnson's face now—only happiness. She looked at the tiny Christmas tree next to her and the nativity scene under its branches, "It's just beautiful," she whispered. Mr. Johnson nodded happily and replied, "In a few hours I will be back, and we will all celebrate Christmas together—now it is time for you to sleep." Without another word, he turned and quietly closed the doors behind him. It wasn't long before Mrs. Johnson and the tiny Christmas tree were sleeping. The worry and pain of the long day had been replaced by a feeling of joy and thankfulness. They both slept peacefully.

The tiny Christmas tree was to have the most wonderful Christmas of all the Christmas trees. In a few hours Mr. Johnson would return to the hospital with Mrs. Johnson's mother and father, his own mother and father, aunts and uncles, and friends. There would be lots of presents, and everyone would say that not only did Mrs. Johnson have a lovely baby, but also the most beautiful Christmas tree they had ever seen. It was to be a Christmas in which all the tiny Christmas tree's hopes and dreams would come true.